JN060181

復興への道—東北の荒れた大地で—

The Way to the Reconstruction
—Upon the Wasted Earth of the Northeast—

浪江町郊外の原発事故の惨状（The miserable state of the nuclear accident of the suburbs of the town of Namie）

福島の春

放射能で汚染された故郷の雪深い山々にも春が忍びより、残雪に映える安達太良や吾妻連峰が早春の空に美しい稜線を描き、秀麗な姿を仰ぎ見ることができる。早春の庭先に咲く可憐な花々が、先行きの見えない前途多難な社会に生きる人びとの不安な心を和ませる。

浪江町の請戸港（Namie's Ukedo Harbor）

The Spring of FUKUSHIMA

Spring creeps up to the snowy mountains of our hometown contaminated by radiation, too. The peaks of Adatara and Azuma lit up in the unmelted snow make up beautiful ridgelines in the sky of early spring. We can command a fine view of the graceful figure. Pretty flowers blooming in the part of the garden in early spring comfort the uneasy heart of the people who live in the society full of difficulties ahead of us.

早春の花見山と吾妻小富士の雪兎
（Hanamiyama in early spring and a varying hare of Azumakofuji）

退職に伴う記念講演
福祉環境学部教授 安藤勝夫
「英文学·英語教育への道」
― 転換期の時代に生きて ―

東日本国際大学退職記念講演（2013年3月）
（My lecture in memory of my retirement from
Higashinippon International University）

オペラ歌手と中欧オペラ公演実行委員会メンバー（Opera singers and members of the exective committee of the opera performance）

オペラ歌手と『魔笛』出演の子供たち
（Opera singers and children who perform "The Magic Flute"）

中欧有数のオペラ歌手ヤナ・ベルナトヴァに促されて『ドン・ジョヴァンニ』の初舞台を踏む。
（I made my first debut on the stage of "Don Jovanni", urged by Yana Bernathova, an eminent opera singer of Central Europe.）

早春賦
Ode to the Early Spring

英詩・英語短歌集
A Collection of English Poems and Tankas

安藤勝夫
ANDO Katsuo

文芸社

A Table of Contents

【第二部】春を待ちつつ2022─故郷の母なる大地で
Waiting for Spring 2022
─ Upon the Mother Earth of our Hometown─

序文　英詩及び英語短歌創作の試み

　筆者は英文学専攻で、主としてハーディの小説や英語教育に関連する論文やエッセイを執筆してきたが、これまで詩や短歌を創作した経験はなく、詩を初めて創作したのは75歳、短歌は80歳になってからである。2011年3月11日に経験した未曾有の東日本大震災と原発事故を題材に初めて詩文を執筆し、年末の挨拶に友人や知人に書き送った。それが思わぬ反響を呼び、各地の世界平和・憲法擁護、脱原発を求める集会で、この詩文を参加者に配布しても良いかとの問い合わせがあり、承諾する旨の手紙を書き送った。

　ところで、世界文学編集委員会から、『世界文学』の特集「災害と文学」に東日本大震災と原発事故に関する原稿執筆の依頼があり、上記の詩文を一部修正し、「原発被災地《福島》からの報告：早春賦─東北の荒れた大地で」を『世界文学』（No.115、2012年7月）に掲載した。

　この報告の中で、大震災と原発事故の大惨事に対する筆者の心情を詩文で執筆した「早春賦2011─東北の荒れた大地で」の約三分の二を英訳し、新英米文学会発行の“New Perspective”（195号、2012年7月）に 'Ode to Early Spring, 2011─Upon the Wasted Earth of the Northeast' という題で掲載した。詩を英訳するに当たって、可能な限り叙事詩（epic）の詩形として使用される blank verse（弱強五歩格iambic pentameter）

の韻律で英訳するように試みた。英詩への造詣が深く、言語的感性の豊かな元福島大学外国人教師ロバート・マーフィ（Robert Murphy）先生は、上記の英詩を「称賛に値するすぐれた詩」（an admirable and fine poem）であると評価したが、彼の示唆に富んだ指摘に従って、英詩を校閲し、必要な修正を行った。

　更に、R. マーフィ先生が、この英詩をフランスのテレビ・ディレクターDominique Balay氏に紹介した。その結果、彼からテレビの「福島特集」で取り上げたいとの要請があった。当時、直ちに渡仏することが困難だったため、テレビのスタジオで録音することができず、その代替措置として、英国在住のマーフィ先生が英詩、安藤が日本語の詩を朗読し、それを吹き込んだテープを送付した。それを基に再編成した英詩がフランスのテレビ番組で放映された。

　当時の勤務先の東日本国際大学特任准教授のノーマン・ダウド氏（英語担当）に、上記の英詩のレビューをお願いしたところ、「早春賦は、悲劇の本質を捉え、作者の意図を表現する」すぐれた詩で、「詩的リズムが流麗である」と評価した。以上のダウド氏の評価が客観的に妥当であるかどうかは、英詩への造詣が深く、言語的感性の豊かな英米人を含む読者の厳正な評価を仰ぎたい。以上の経緯を経て、この英詩を『新英語教育』に投稿し、13連（stanza）137行の長編詩の一部の3連28行を「震災詩（英訳詩）創作の試み」として『新英語教育』（2012年10月、三友社出版）に掲載した。

筆者はこれまで短歌を詠んだ経験がない門外漢であるが、以上の英詩創作の経験を踏まえて、今度は短歌の韻律を踏まえた英語短歌の創作を試みた。これまで創作した短歌はいずれも、素人の歌心・詩的情緒に乏しい作品であるが、初めて詠んだ短歌を試みに「朝日歌壇」に投稿したところ、幸運にも馬場あき子選で入選し、朝日新聞（2017年4月17日）に掲載された。この短歌とその後に詠んだ短歌3首を英訳し、『新英語教育』（2020年1・2月号）に掲載した。その後、主として東日本大震災と原発事故、現今の危機的政治状況、若き日の思い出を題材に76首の短歌を詠み、英訳したが、公表する機会がなかった。これまで未公表だった短歌を秦野市の広報誌『緑のはだの』に掲載することになった。その契機となったのは、福島大学の教え子の木村澄子さんが、「朝日歌壇」選者の馬場あき子の門下生で歌集を7冊刊行している下田市在住の歌人・長友くにさんに紹介する労を取ったことである。

　最近、これまで詠んだ短歌100首を英訳し、「春を待ちつつ2022」（Waiting for Spring, 2022）として纏めた。これまでも自作の詩や短歌が英訳された例はあるが、私の知る限り、叙事詩（epic）や短歌の韻律で英訳した例はないのではないかと思う。この意味では、新しい試みであるといえる。前述したように、"New Perspective"には約三分の二を英訳し掲載したが、今回、書籍として纏めるに当たって、残りの三分の一を英訳し、完成した。なお、読者の方々には、叙事詩の韻律で創作した「早春賦2011―東北の荒れた大地で」（Ode to Early Spring 2011

—Upon the Wasted Earth of the Northeast）と短歌の韻律を
踏まえた英語短歌をお読みいただき、忌憚のないご意見・ご感
想をお寄せ戴ければ幸いである。

【Preface】My Attempt to Create English Poems and Tankas

I specialize in English literature and have written some theses
with special reference to Hardy's novel and English education. I
have never experienced in the creation of poetry and tanka. For
the first time at seventy-five years of age I created English poem,
and eighty years old I composed English tankas. I wrote prose and
poetry about the unprecedented great earthquake of Eastern Japan and the nuclear accident for the first time, and I sent them to
my close friends and acquaintances. These aroused unexpected
responses, and I received several inquiries about whether they
distributed this poetry or not. I sent them my response that I
agreed to it.

By the way, the editorial committee of "World Literature" requested me to write the contribution about the great earthquake
of Eastern Japan and the nuclear accident in the special number of
the disaster and literature. I corrected a part of the above-men-
tioned prose and poetry, and published 'my report from Fukushima' written in Japanese, the disaster-stricken area of the nuclear
accident: 'Ode to Early Spring 2011—Upon the Wasted Earth of
the Northeast' in "World Literature" (No.115, July 2012). In this report, I translated into English about two-thirds of 'Ode to Early
Spring 211—Upon the Wasted Earth of the Northeast' in which I

wrote my feelings for the highly destructive disaster of the great earthquake and the nuclear accident, and I published it in this title in "New Perspective" (No.195, July 2012). I tried to put this poem as much as possible in the meter of blank verse (iambic pentameter) used as poetic form of epic. Prof. Robert Murphy who has a profound knowledge of English poetry and an ample sensibility of language estimated this poem as 'an admirable and fine poem.' According to his advice, I checked this poem and carried out the necessary corrections of it.

Moreover, Prof. Robert Murphy introduced this poem to Mr. Dominique Balay, French TV Director. As its result, he proposed that he wanted to take up this poem in the special TV program of Fukushima. As it was difficult to go to France soon at that time, we could not record the poem we read at the studio of TV. As this alternative measure, Prof. Murphy read this English poem, and Ando read Japanese poem, and each one recorded them on the tape. We sent them to Mr. D. Balay. The English poem which was rearranged on the basis of it was telecasted in the French TV program.

I requested Mr. Norman Dowd, Associate Prof. of Higashinippon International University to estimate this poem. He pointed out, 'Ode to Early Spring is the excellent poem which captures the essence of tragedy and expresses the intention of the author, and its poetic rhythm flows elegantly.' About whether his estimation is to the point or not, I want to receive the strict estimation by the British or Americans who have affluent linguistic sensibility.

I am a layman who has not composed any tanka, but on the basis of my experience of creating the English poem, I tried to create English tanks in the meter of a tanka. All the tankas that I created lack in poetic disposition or poetic emotion, but I tried to contribute to 'Asahikadan' the tanka which I composed for the first time. Fortunately, it was chosen by Akiko Baba, a judge of 'Asahikadan', and it was published in the newspaper of Asahi (July 17, 2017). I translated into English this tanka and three tankas which I composed afterwards, and published them in the magazine of "The New English Classroom" (January & February, 2020). Afterwards, I composed 76 tankas and put them into English chiefly in the theme of the great earthquake of Eastern Japan, the nuclear accident and the dangerous political situation at present and my memories of younger days. I published my unpublished tankas in "Midori no Hadano", the Information Bulletin of Hadano city. Its motive was that Ms. Sumiko Kimura, my student of Fukushima University, took the trouble to introduce them to Mrs. Kuni Nagatomo, a disciple of Akiko Baba, a judge of 'Asahikadan', and a poetess who published seven collections of tankas.

Recently, I have translated into English one hundred tankas which I composed until now, and organized them as 'Waiting for Spring, 2022'. There are some examples that one's own poems and tankas were put into English, but as far as I know, I think there is no example that one's own poem and tankas were translated into English in the meter of epic or tanka. In this sense, it may be said that it is a new attempt. I expect all readers to read 'Ode to Early Spring, 2011!' and English tankas.I am fortunate to give me your frank opinions and impressions about them.

第一部

早春賦2011—東北の荒れた大地で—

Ode to Early Spring, 2011
— Upon the Wasted Earth of the Northeast —

早春賦2011―東北の荒れた大地で―

1 プロローグ

戦争の悪夢から覚めて六十有余年
年月の足音を刻みながら幾度か巡りくる春
2011年新春―
夜明けを待ちながら　瞳を凝らし
耳を澄ます　その厳冬の闇の奥から
明日を告げる夜明けの鼓動が遠く近く聞こえ始める
凍てついた大地のいたる所に春の気配が漂う
厳冬を縫って忍び寄ってくる
春のせせらぎの言葉に耳を傾けようとする
熱い衝動をもう抑えることができない

2　早春を迎えて

立春が過ぎ　3月を迎えて
故郷の雪深い山々にも春が忍びより
残雪に映える安達太良や吾妻連峰が
早春の空に美しい稜線を描き
秀麗な姿を仰ぎ見ることができる
早春の庭先に咲く可憐な花々が
前途多難な社会に生きる人びとの
不安な心を和ませる

東北の空には灰色の雲が重く垂れ込め
街路樹が冷たい早春の微風にそよぎ
その心を覗きみることはできなかったが
街を行く人びとの表情も心なしか暗い
市街に林立する「がんばろう！福島」の旗が
春風にそよぎ　咽び泣いていた

3 東日本大震災と原発事故

2011年3月11日—
肌寒い早春の昼下がり2時46分
突如　家がドシーンと強く大きく揺れ
途方もない強い振動が地響きのように長く続いた
家具が倒れ　食器が壊れ　本が書斎に散乱した
24時間停電　1週間断水　ガスが使用不能
テレビの画面が消え　正確な情報が途絶えた

大震災後　落ち着く暇もなく
3月12日午後3時36分
第一原発1号機水素爆発
続いて14日午前11時頃　3号機水素爆発
15日午前6時10分　2号機爆発音
4号機火災が発生し　炉心溶融して
次々と水素爆発を起こし
福島の空に大量の放射性物質を拡散した

巨大地震と大津波の生々しい爪跡が
テレビの画面に次々と映し出される
水素爆発で崩壊した三つの原子炉建屋
廃墟と化した市街地　大量の瓦礫の山
破壊された美しい自然と故郷
倒壊した家の前で茫然自失する人びと
瓦礫越しに見える静かな海を見つめる老漁夫
亡骸にすがって泣き崩れる母子の姿
言葉に尽くせない惨状が胸に迫る
放射能被曝危険値をはるかに超える危険区域で
醜悪な残骸を晒す建屋に放水する消防隊員
重装備の防護服をまとって作業する下請け労働者
瓦礫の中で行方不明者を探索する自衛隊員
大震災の惨状を伝える鮮烈な映像が胸を抉る
生命の危険を厭わず働く人びとの献身的な姿に
原発事故に苦しむ住民は苦渋の涙を流す

4　原発被災地・福島市の状況

　３月15日の福島市内の放射能平均測定値は

18時の１時間平均23.188を最高に

翌日は１時間20超マイクロシーベルト

この日一日の行動でどれだけ放射能を被曝したか

原因不明の筋肉痛と腰痛を治療するため

病院への通院に要した時間が往復30分

トイレ用の水を川で汲みあげる作業に１時間半

食料と乾電池・灯油など当面の必需品を

買い求めるのに要した時間１時間半

飲料水を汲みに行った知人宅の井戸の前には

長い列ができ　飲料水を確保するのに30分

この日屋外で過ごした時間は都合4時間
80マイクロシーベルトを超える放射能被曝
ここ数日断水で入浴用の水が確保できず
放射能を洗い落とせないまま身体に蓄積した
原発事故後何日も支援物資が被災地に届かず
わずかな食料・水・必需品を求めて
車にガソリンが補給できるか不確かなまま
スーパーマーケットやガソリンスタンドに
人や車の長蛇の列ができた

5　安全神話の捏造と崩壊

政府当局・東電は大本営発表さながらに
事故の真の原因を隠蔽したまま
原発事故は大津波による想定外の事故だと強弁した
テレビでは放射能の測定値をテロップで流し
原子力安全・保安委員が能面のような表情で
現段階では「直ちに人体に影響を及ぼさない」
「Ｘ線検査で放射線400マイクロシーベルト被曝」
と大本営発表をオウム返しに繰り返し
新たな放射能安全神話の捏造に狂奔する

半径20キロ圏内から30キロ圏内を機械的に
避難・屋内退避・緊急時避難準備区域に設定し
14万人の住民に避難・屋内退避を指示する
避難区域内に居住する対象住民は21万人余
県外への避難希望者３万数千人
避難した「原発難民」７万数千人
半径５キロ圏内の住民に避難命令が出たが
避難する目的地の当てもなく
着のみ着のままで各地に避難
福島市郊外の運動公園の体育館には数百人避難
毛布１枚・水１本・おにぎり１個配給
寝場所には仕切りがなく
予想を超える過酷な避難生活が待ち受けていた

6　放射能差別と風評被害

原発の安全神話が崩れ　何も信じられず
放射能への不安と恐怖だけが募った
為政者の無為・無策　根拠のない情報が
放射能差別を生み出し
風評被害を拡大再生産した
福島産・福島出身というだけで
酪農家が手塩にかけて飼育した牛が
何千頭も放置されたまま　餓死し屠殺された
被災地では食糧が不足する一方で
大量の原乳・野菜が大量に投棄された
結婚適齢期の若い娘が婚約を破棄され
転校先の学校では「放射能をうつすな
撒き散らすな」とはやし立てられた
福島ナンバーの車が給油・駐車を拒否され
県外に避難した人々がホテルの宿泊を断られ
心ない差別的言動が口から口へ伝えられた

県内の温泉地では予約が次々とキャンセルされ
訪れる客もなく　近隣の温泉地では避難者が
旅館の片隅でひっそりと肩を寄せ合っていた
岳・土湯温泉の老舗旅館が何軒も倒産し
土産店など関連企業がそれに続いた
被災地での無償のボランティア活動や
全国からの善意の救援物資が届けられたが
その一方で風評被害が全国に広がっていった

7　原発事故から20日後（３月31日）の惨状

死者１万1532人　行方不明者１万6441人
東北全体の避難者40万3800人余
放射能汚染で立ち入り禁止された地域では
行方不明者が数多く瓦礫と泥水に晒され
その霊を弔い悼む機会すらなかった
原発事故は収束する見通しが立たず
立ち入り禁止・緊急避難準備区域の住民７万人余
故郷・家・田畑・生活の場を奪われたまま
北は北海道から南は沖縄の全国各地へ
福島県内の放射能汚染の少ない市町村へ避難した
県外へ避難した児童・生徒数は８千数百人
県内の他校へ転校した生徒も3000人を超え
居住地に残った児童・生徒は
屋外での運動・活動・遊びを禁止、抑制された

巨大地震・大津波・原発事故が引き起こした
福島県内の4月末現在の甚大な被害の数々——
県内の死者3241人　行方不明者1432人
児童・生徒約3700名が福島県外へ避難・転校
学級数約3700クラスの減少が予想されるため
公立小中学校の今年度教員採用試験中止決定
常磐線いわき市久ノ浜駅から宮城県亘理駅まで全面運休
駅の大部分が立ち入り禁止・避難区域となった
大津波で駅舎流失・線路破損のため
復旧の見通し立たず　原町・相馬駅からバス代行運転
いわき市の水族館アクアマリンふくしまの
世界の海・河川に棲息する魚類2万数千匹全滅
家屋・道路・漁港・堤防・漁船等の倒壊、破損
農業・酪農・畜産業・漁業・商工業・医療
原発事故の風評被害を受けた中小の観光事業
旅館・旅行代理店・バス会社など
被害総額は数千億円に上る天文学的数値で、統計上未確定

8　大震災 6 カ月後の福島県の現状

大震災・原発事故後の福島県の現状は次の通り——

総人口　震災前224万401人（3月1日時点）

　震災後199万7400人（7月1日時点）

避難者数　県内3942人（9月6日時点）

　県外46都道府県5万5793人（8月25日時点）

警戒区域（半径20キロ圏内立ち入り禁止）

　浪江・双葉・大熊・富岡・楢葉・葛尾 6 町村

　南相馬市の一部　対象住民約 3 万1800人

緊急時避難準備区域

（30キロ圏内で事態急変の場合の退避・退避準備区域）

　広野町全域　南相馬・田村・楢葉・川内の

　5 市町村の一部　対象住民約 5 万8500人

　避難住民約 2 万8000人

計画的避難区域——50キロ圏内の放射能汚染の現状

　飯舘村住民のほぼ全員が居住する川俣町山木屋地区

　年間積算放射線量年間20ミリシーベルト超

児童生徒（小中高生）・幼稚園児

　　震災前の在籍数　約27万人（2010年）

　　震災後の転校・転園　約１万8000人

児童生徒の県内外への転校　１万596人

　　県外への転校　9880人（夏休み終了時）

　　県内での転校　6066人（夏休み終了時）

避難区域内相双地区８高校の実態

　　相双地区８高校は県内各地の24高校に分散

　　サテライト方式の授業実施　受講者数1889人

外国人観光客　約94.6％減少（４・７月比）

　　震災前（2019）3239人　震災後（2011）174人

コメの作付面積　約19.1％減少

　　震災前８万6000ha　震災後６万5200ha

モモの価格　約55.4％下落（１kg当たり）

　　震災前437円　震災後195円（１kg当たり）

和牛の価格　約37.5％下落（１kg当たり）

　　震災前1737円　震災後1035円（１kg当たり）

9　原発事故への住民の要求

放射能汚染地域の全住民が「安心して暮らせる
生活環境を取り戻すため　放射能を徹底的に
除染せよ！」の切実な声が沸き起こる
原発事故以来　放射能への不安を募らせつつ
大震災の衝撃から落ち着きを取り戻し
住民が各地で自主的に放射能学習会開催
どの会場も主催者の予想を超える参加者数
大震災に備えて原発の安全策を講ずるよう
訴訟を進めてきた弁護士　反原発の住民運動に
献身してきた人びと　放射能防護学・放射線医学・
原子核物理学の専門家に講師依頼
幼児・児童を抱える若い母親の参加が目立つ
幼子・乳飲み子を抱えて一旦は夫と別居し県外に避難
悩んだ末福島に戻り　家族の絆を深めながら
頑張ろうと再決意した若い母親の悲痛な訴えが
参加者の心を打ち　奮い立たせた

子どもが安全に通学し学習できるように
住民が安心して日常生活が送れるように
学校・公園・住宅地の放射線量を測定し
年間被曝線量１ミリシーベルト以下に抑え
「放射能除染を徹底せよ」との住民の要望が高まる
市町村は住民の切実な声に押されて重い腰を上げ
除染作業に着手・推進し
すべての学校の除染がほぼ完了した
町内会ごとに住民が自主的に住宅の放射線の測定実施
放射線量の高い福島市市街地の渡利等三地区では
粘り強い除染を要請する住民運動が続いた

10　巨大地震と原発事故に立ち向かい
　　　　豊かな生活を再生するために

人類史上最悪の大惨事の第二次世界大戦以来
経験したことのない大災害が人心を揺るがし
巨大地震と大津波が東北の大地を襲い
原発事故が福島の空に放射性物質を撒き散らし
故郷の豊かな大地を荒地に変えた

瓦礫と廃虚の中から
奪われた故郷から
汚染された荒地から
瓦礫に埋もれた魂の苦悶を
生き残った者の悲痛な叫びを
限りなく流れた涙の礫を
どう言葉に紡ぎ出せばいいのか

原子力の平和利用の名のもとに
日米安保体制の強化に狂奔する
国家権力の黒い意図を覆い隠し
巨額の札束と宣伝を総動員し
捏造した安全神話を振りかざして

原発利権に群がる欺瞞者を暴き出し
権益が集中する原子力ムラの牙城に
どう切り込み告発すればいいのか

目に見えぬ放射能の恐怖に怯え
別れて暮らす夫の身を案じ
将来の生活に思いを馳せる母親に
生まれたばかりの乳飲み子の頰を
あふれる涙で濡らしながら
子どもの将来を案じる若い母親に
育ち盛りの子どもが外で遊べず
閉め切った部屋の片隅で
一日中ゲームに興じる子どもに苛立ち
抑え切れぬ怒りをぶつける母親に
切り裂かれた家族の絆を取り戻し
家族が一緒に生活できるように
どう援助の手を差し伸べればいいのか

農漁民が安全な食材を提供し
子どもを放射能の内部被曝から守り

汚染地域の住民の健康を維持し
正常な生活を取り戻せるように
汚染地域の放射能を徹底的に除染し
地域住民の信頼の絆で結ばれた
新しい共同社会を再建するために
どう力を合わせればいいのか

氾濫する情報の渦の中から
欺瞞と捏造・偽善を抉り出し
虚偽と絶望を真実と希望の言葉に
差別と分断を平等と連帯の砦に
荒廃と廃虚を実りと豊穣の大地に
どうつくり変えればいいのか

災害に苦しむ人びとの声に耳を傾け
悲しみに沈む人びとの心を奮い立たせ
ばらばらになった人びとの心を結びつけ
信じ合う人びとの絆を強め
働く人びとに連帯の輪を広げ
人間らしい豊かな生活の再生へと
どう結びつけていけばいいのか

美しい自然と故郷を
働き生きる場を取り戻し
人間らしく生きる生活を
新たに再生するために
私たちの心の叫びを
その言葉の礫を解き放ち
悲しみと怒りを力にして
東北の荒れた大地に
新しい歌声よ　おこれ！

11 エピローグ

厳しい冬の時代にあってもなお
春先の花々の芽が
深い根雪の下に芽生えるように
私たちの営みは春の兆しの中で鍛えられる
私たちは今日も歌う　私たちの冬
この国の厳しい冬を突き破る歌を
今日も私たちは歌おう
凍てついた大地の至る所で
尽きることのない春の泉を汲みとれるように
豊かな明日への飛躍に向けて
厳しい冬を突き破る歌を
未来を拓く夜明けの歌を
声を合わせて共に歌おう
東北の荒れた大地で私たちの春を
豊かに花開かせるために！

無人の富岡町「夜ノ森」の桜並木
(A row of cherry blossoms in 'Yonomori' of Tomioka
uninhabited in this area)

Ode to Early Spring, 2011
— Upon the Wasted Earth of the Northeast —

1. Prologue

Awaking from the nightmare of the war,
Upward of sixty years have passed away.
The New Year 2011 has come—
Their steps reverberate as they approach,
Yet, we anticipate returning spring.
And waiting for the day to break anew
From gloomy depths of this harsh winter's day,
We note, with eyes and ears full-straining now,
The pulse of dawn that heralds coming day
Begins to beat both near and far away.
All over now, beneath the frozen earth
Slight signs of spring are trembling in the air.
We can no more control our hearty urge
To hear more closely this sweet babble of spring
That creeps upon us through the intense cold.

2. Hailing Early Spring

The first signs of spring passed and turned to March,
Spring crept up in the snowy mountains, too.
The peaks of Adatara and Azuma
Which were lit up by the unmelted snow
Looked in bold relief in the sky of early spring,
And grey and heavy clouds were hanging now.
We could command a fine view of graceful figure
Across the skies that covered the northeast.
Pretty flowers which bloomed in the garden
Comforted the uneasy heart of the people
Who lived in the hard society ahead.

The grey clouds hang in the sky of the Northeast
The roadside trees were rustling now and then
In a breeze that chilled, of early spring.
Although I could not look into their hearts,
The looks of the passers-by in the street
Were also somehow a little dark.
The flags "Let's do our best!" brisling in the street
Were fluttering and sobbing in the spring's wind.

3. The Great Earthquake and the Nuclear Accident

The eleventh of March, twenty-eleven
In early afternoon, that chilly spring,
At forty-six past two, just then, oh, then,
I suddenly felt the house strongly convulsed.
A massive quake, it thudded on and on!
So much collapsing furniture, smashing crockery,
So many books were hurled about the room.
So many broken roof-tiles, walls in chunks,
The power failed, lay dormant for a day,
Supplies of water cut off for a week,
And severed, too, reliable information
As TV screens were rendered blank and mute.

One day, the twelfth, after this monster quake,
The first atomic plant disaster happened,
The afternoon, it was, three thirty-six:
The first reactor melted down and caused
A hydrogen explosion, followed then
By Numbers 3, and 2, and 4.
A high degree of radio-active substances
Were scattered through the skies of Fukushima.

The wakes of the huge quake and tidal wave
Were described one and after in the screen of TV.
The three buildings of nuclear reactors

Which crumbled by the hydrogen's explosion.
The urban district which was devastated.
A great amount of a heat of rubbles.
Beautiful nature and hometown destroyed.
The people who were stunned before their house
The old fisher who gazed on the silent sea
Which could be seen through a lot of debris.
The figure of the mother and her child
Who burst into tears over their dead corpes.
The undescribed wretched scene touched our hearts.
In the risky zone which surpass by far
The risk of radiation exposure
Fire brigades who release so much water
Buildings which expose the ugly wreckages.
The subcontractors who work wearing
Protective clothes of heavy equipment.
Self-Defense Force officials who look for
The missing persons in debris and rubble.
The vivid screen images which deliver
The disastrous scenes pierce our hearts strongly.
The dwellers who suffer from the nuclear accidents
Shed their bitter tears moved so deeply by
The figures of people who work selflessly
Without minding the danger of their lives.

4. The Present situation of Fukushima city, The Disaster-stricken Area of Nuclear Power Plants

The Average measured value of radiation
Of Fukushima City on March 15
23.188 micro-sieverts on the average an hour
On the maximum at 18 o'clock
On the next day twenty super-micro-sieverts
Of radio activity an hour.
How much radiation was I exposed to
Only by my activity this day?
It took 30 minutes to go to and from hospital
To treat my muscular and lower-back pain
Caused by its unknown etiology.
It took an hour and half to draw water
In the river used for our toilets.
And an hour and half to buy essential goods
Including food, dry batteries and fuel.
Many people lined up in front of the well
Of my acquaintance to pump drinks we needed,
So It took thirty minutes to secure water,
I spent outdoors for four hours this day.
So I was exposed to radiation
Above eighty micro-sieverts on this day.
These several days I could not secure
Water necessary for taking baths.

Because of suspension of water supply
Radiation stored up in my body
Vital goods for support had not arrived
To the zone which suffered from disaster.
For some days after nuclear accident
Lots of people and cars formed a long line
Searching for food, water and essential goods
In front of supermarkets and service stations
Being not sure if they could supply gasoline.

5. The Fabrication and Breakdown of a Myth About the Safety of Nuclear Power Plants

The government Authorities and Toden
Concealed the true cause of the accident
And insisted that the nuclear accident
Was caused by the great tsunami
Which we were not able to imagine
The estimated amount of radiation.
TV threw the estimated amount
Of radiation by the projector
The Nuclear Safety Commission
Repeated the announcement of
The Imperial Headquarter like a parrot.
'It won't inflict an injury on the human body'
And was exposed to radiation of
400 micro-sieberts by X-ray inspection
And rushed madly about the new fabrication
Of myth about the safety of radiation.

The Government Authority and Toden
Set up the area of the Refuge,
Evacuation indoors and
The Preparation for emergency
And indicated the refuge or
Indoor evacuation to the dwellers
Of a hundred and forty thousands.
The inhabitants who were the objects

Of living within the zone of the refuge
Were the rest of twenty-one hundred thousands.
Thirty thousands and several thousands of people
Hoped to take refuge outside the Prefecture.
Refugees who evacuated to
The other zone by the nuclear accident
Were seventy and several thousands.
The Authority ordered 'Take refuge
To the dwellers who lived within a radius
Of ten kilometers,' but they took refuge
To each part of the country in Japan.
With no special destination in mind
And with nothing but the clothes on their back
Hundreds of people evacuated
In Gymnasium for athletic sports
In the suburbs of Fukushima.
A blanket, a bottle of water and
A rice ball were distributed to them.
No partition was in the place to sleep
Severe life awaited evacuees
So far beyond their anticipation.

6. The Distinction Caused by Radioactivity And Damages Caused by Rumors

The myth of the safety of nuclear power plants
Was broken down, so residents couldn't believe
Anything and increased only their anxieties
And fears of radioactivity.
Idleness, lack of policy and groundless information
Of politicians brought forth the distinction
Caused by Radioactivity and
Expanded and reproduced damages by rumors.
Thousands of cows bred by dairy farmers
With great care starved to death
Only because they were produced in or
Came from Fukushima prefecture
They were slaughtered without any meaning.
While there wasn't enough food in the stricken zone,
Great amount of original milk and vegetables
Were abandoned without utilization.
Young women of marriageable age
Were broken off engagement one-sidedly.
Transfer pupils were jeered in their changing schools,
"Don't infect nor scatter about radiation."
Cars with Fukushima license plates
Were refused oil absorption and parking.
The people who evacuated outside the prefecture
Were refused their stay at hotel and

Discriminable words and behaviors
Spread to many people by word of mouth.

A hotel reservation was cancelled one after another
In the spa within the prefecture and
There were no visitors to the spring-spa.
Refugees stayed shoulder to shoulder silently
In the corner of the hotel or inn.
Several long-established inns or hotels
Of the spas of Dake and Tsuchiyu
Were bankrupted one after another and
Companies closely related to them
And souvenir shops continued to go down.
Volunteer activities in the stricken zone
And relief supplies from the whole country
Were delivered with good intention,
And on the other hand a lot of damages
Caused by rumors spread to all the countries.

7. The Disastrous Scene of Twenty days After the Nuclear Accidents

The dead were 11,532 persons, and
The number of persons missing was 16,441.
The refugees of the Northeast in total
Were more than 405,800.
In an off-limit zone polluted with radiation
Lots of missing persons were exposed
With a heap of debris and muddy water,
And had even no chance of mourning the soul.
It was so difficult to have the prospects
That the nuclear accident would return to normal.
There were more than seventy thousands of residents
Residents more than seventy thousands
Living in the restricted area and
In the district in which they prepared for
Their emergency evacuation
Were robbed of their native place, residence,
Rice and vegetable field and their place of life,
And evacuated all areas of the country
From Hokkaido to Okinawa,
And cities, towns and villages which have
A small quantity of radioactive contamination
Within Fukushima Prefecture.
Eight thousand and several hundreds of pupils
And schoolchildren evacuated outside the prefecture.
Schoolchildren more than three thousands also

Changed to another schools within the prefecture.
School children and pupils who remained
In their place of residence were prohibited
And restrained from physical exercises,
Activities and plays out of doors.

The great earthquake, the gigantic tsunami
And the nuclear accident brought about
A large number of enormous damages
As of the end of April within Fukushima Prefecture.
The dead persons within the prefecture
Were 3,241, and the missing persons were 1,432.
Schoolchildren and pupils of 3,700
Evacuated and changed their schools
Outside Fukushima Prefecture.
About a hundred classes were expected
To decrease, so the employment test of teachers
Of a public primary and middle school
Was decided to be suspended this year.
Train service was totally suspended
From the station of Iwaki-Hisanohama
Of the Joban Line to Watari station
Of Miyagi Prefecture. It was forbidden
To enter the most part of the station,
Which became the zone of evacuation.

Because of the loss of the station building
And the damage of the railway tracks,
The prospect of recovery couldn't be made,
So the bus ran in place of the train.
Twenty and several thousands of fishes
Were exterminated, which lived in the sea
And rivers of the world which was controlled
By Aquarium Fukushima of Iwaki city.
The destruction and damage of houses,
Roads, fishing ports and boats, dikes and so on.
Agriculture, dairy and livestock industry, fishing industry
Commerce and industry, and medical treatment.
The central and small tourist industry,
Inns and hotels, travel agencies and
Bus companies, which took damages
Caused by Rumors of the nuclear accident.
The total amount of damages was
Astronomical figure which counted
Several hundred billions and not yet settled
According to the statistics.

8. The Present Situation of Fukushima Prefecture Of Six Months after the Great Earthquake

The present situation of Fukushima
Prefecture after the great earthquake and
Nuclear accident was as follows;
The total population was 2,204,401.
Before the great earthquake (as of March 1).
   1,997,400 people after the great earthquake (as of June 1).
   The number of evacuees was
   3,942 people within the prefecture (as of September 6)
   55,793 people; 46 prefectures of Japan (as of August 25)
Area of caution (An off-limits area within a 20-kilometer radius)
   6 towns and villages: Namie, Futaba, Okuma, Tomioka, Katsuo
   A part of Minami-Soma city
   Residents of its Subject are about 31.800 people.

The area of preparation for evacuation in case of emergency
(The area of evacuation and the area of preparation for evacuation
   Within a radius of 30 kilometers)
   The whole area of Hirono Town,
   A part of five cities towns and villages
   Of Minamisoma, Tamura, Naraha and Kawauhi
   The residents of a target are about 58,500 people
   The residents of evacuation are about 28, 000 people.

Planned area of evacuation —The present situation of
    Radioactive contamination within 50 kilometers
    Yamakiya's district of Kawamata town where
    Nearly all the residents of Iidate village reside
    Nearly accumulated amount of radioactivity
    was super-twenty sieverts
Primary schoolchildren, middle school students
    Kindergarteners enrolled before the earthquake
    Were about twenty-seven hundreds of people (2010).
    Changing of schools and kindergartens after the earthquake
    Were about eighteen thousands of pupils.
    Changing of schools inside and outside the prefecture
    Changing schools outside the prefecture were.

Nine thousands, eight hundreds and eighty
(At the time of finishing summer vacation)
Changing schools inside and outside the prefecture
Changing schools outside the prefecture were
Eight thousands and sixty.
Changing schools inside the prefecture were
Six thousands and sixty-eight pupils
(At the time of finishing summer vacation)
The actual condition of eight high schools

In the Soso's area inside the evacuation area
Eight high schools of Soso's area dispersed
Twenty-four high schools of the searchlight form
Of each area within the prefecture and
Carrying out the teaching form of searchlight
Whose students who attended it were 1,888 students.
Foreign tourists decreased to 94.6 percentages
(Compared with April and July).
3,236 persons before the earthquake (2010)
3,239 persons after the earthquake (2911).
The area of the planting of rice
Were reduced to about 19.1 percentages.
86, 000 hectares before the earthquake
65,200 hectares after the earthquake.

The price of peaches was reduced to
About 55.4 percentage. (per one kilogram),
437 yen before the earthquake
195 yen after the earthquake (per one kilogram)
The price of a Japanese bread of cow
Reduced to 55 percentage (per one kilogram).
1,737yen before the earthquake.
1,085 yen after the earthquake (per one kilogram).

9. The Demand of Residents Towards the Nuclear Accidents

The urgent voices rose up earnestly,
"Remove radiation so completely
In order that all the people living
In the zone polluted by radiation
Might recover the good circumstance of
Our life in which they can live in safety!"
Since the nuclear plant accident occurred
The residents let their apprehension
Increase their anxieties to radiation,
And restored their stability themselves
From their shock of the destructive earthquake.
They held their meeting voluntarily
To learn about radio activity.
In all the halls were more participants
Than most promoters anticipated.
Lawyers sued for taking a safe measure
For radiation against the great earthquake.
The people dedicated themselves to
Residents' campaign against nuclear power plants
And asked a lecturer to an expert of
Radiology, radiation physics
And protection scholarship of nuclear physics.
Lots of young mothers who hold their Infants
And children in their arms take part in this movement.
Holding their suckling and children in their arms

Live separately apart from their husband
And evacuated outside prefecture once.
After they worried about whither they came home
They returned home to Fukushima once,
And the sorrowful appeals of young mother
Who made up her mind to hold out again
Deeping familial ties appealed to
And bestirred the hearts of participants.
So that children may go to school safely
And so that they may study at school again,
So that dwellers may live their daily life
Feeling at ease without their anxieties,
They measured the amount of radiation
And control radiation exposure
Below one mille-siebert all year round,
The demand of residents were intensified
'Decontaminate radiation thoroughly.'
Municipalities were urged upon
By the serious voices of residents,
And got to their heavy feet finally,
Set about, promoted and almost completed
Decontamination of all the schools.
Residents carried out the measurement
Of radioactivity of dwellings voluntarily
In the neighboring association.

In the three districts including Watari
Of the urban districts of Fukushima
With the high amount of radiation
A persistent residents' campaign continued
Which demanded decontamination.

10. To Restore Our Rich Life Fighting against
The Enormous Earthquake and The Nuclear Accidents

Since World War II's long-drawn-out end arrived,
The worst disaster we've experienced
Has shaken the hearts of people in Japan.
Unleashed with that unprecedented earthquake,
Succeeded by the giant tsunami
That smashed Eastern Japan's Pacific coast,
Until the nuclear accident scattered wide
A host of radio-active substances
Across the skies of vast Fukushima,
And made of that rich soil a wasted land.

From a million heaps of debris, countless ruins,
From each native place we were deprived of,
From such contaminated, wasted earth,
The agonies of souls buried in ruins,
The bitter cries of grief of those surviving,
The endless flow of tears out of the stones,
How shall we spin adequate words from them?

Authority conceals its evil will,
And runs amok to bolster up the system of
US-Japan security in the name
Of peaceful uses of atomic power,
Lifting the veil that hides such fraudulent people,

Who spout again that myth they forged, of 'safety',
And read from huge amounts of copious notes,
Trying to mobilize the media,
To form again the swarms that will uphold,
Shore up the vested rights of nuclear plants.
Against the 'atomic village' in such citadels
On which all rights and interests converge
How shall we breach and accuse its power?

To the Mother who is riven by the fear
Of those invisible radio-active substances,
Who fears for a husband now living apart,
And weeps and wets with overflowing tears
Both cheeks of the suckling newly-born to this,
That seeps henceforth into the child's whole life;
To the Mother nettled with rage and who betrays
Her motherly anger to the growing child,
No longer able to play in the open air,
And yet absorbed in playing in the corner
Of a room with every window closed all day;
To the Mother whose family have left their old home
Polluted with radio-active substances,
And now are forced to spend their lives as refugees,
That Mother now yearning to have restored
Those ties of blood to the stable life they led:

How shall we give our hands to such Mothers?

For food that is reliable, secure,
Provided by our fishermen, our farmers;
To shield our children, now exposed to radiation,
And others living in polluted zones,
To help them all maintain the best of health,
Regain that normal life that is their due;
That decontamination be promoted
Exhaustively in all polluted zones;
That residents of places now uprooted
May soon rebuild their smashed communities
With bonds of friendship, bonds of mutual trust:
How shall we work together to these ends?

And now, from swirling floods of information,
To dredge deceit, hypocrisy, fabrication,
To change despair and lies to hope and truth.
To change discrimination and disunion
To equality and solidarity
And so restore our wasted, ruined earth,
Return it to a ripening, fertile land:
In our capacity as human beings,
How shall we act to best attain these ends?

By listening seriously to the words of those
Who suffer from the great disaster still,
By rallying spirits of those so mired in grief;
Linking the hearts of those left disengaged,
Deepening the ties of those rich in belief;
Widening the circle of bonds with working people,
Widening access to rich and human life:
How can we forge the bonds to link our people?

Restoring nature, places we called home,
Society where we can work and live,
To generate anew our lives as humans,
Let's throw, not stones, but words and hearty cries,
Channeling the grief and anger in our hearts,
And raise our range of voices in new songs
Upon the wasted earth of the northeast.

11. Epilogue

No matter how harsh winter's times may be,
As sprouts of flowers sprung in early spring,
Awake beneath the deeply rooted snow
Our life is fostered in the signs of spring.
Let's sing again our winter's song today
And draw from underneath the frozen earth
The ceaseless, affluent fountain of our spring
To break the intense winter of this land.
Just like the earth to help awaken spring,
Intently leap to coming days of hope,
Let's sing our song of dawn in chorus fine,
To help us pioneer our future days,
That spring in all its prime might fully bloom
Upon the wasted earth of the northeast!

第二部

春を待ちつつ2022—故郷の母なる大地で

Waiting for spring 2022
— Upon the Mother Earth of our Hometown—

1. 春を待ちつつ 2022

Waiting for spring 2022

原発の事故の傷痕なお深く
荒れた大地に忍び寄る春

> The massive scars caused
> By the nuclear accident
> Are still fathomless
> Yet spring creeps up on the earth
> Wasted by the disaster

春を呼ぶ吾妻に映える雪兎
人無き里に桜綻ぶ

> Snow-Hare calling spring
> Looks lovely in bold relief
> In Azuma's breast
> Cherry blossoms start blooming
> In the deserted hometown

白波の寄せる岸辺に春遠く
瓦礫の街に人影ぞなき

      The white-crested waves
      Were surging on the seashore
      Spring was far away
      In the debris-scattered street
      Not a soul was to be seen

復興の掛け声むなし被災地の
全面除染遅々と進まず

      In the stricken zone
      A cry for restoration
      Sounds ineffective
      All decontamination
      Progresses at a snail's pace

原発の事故の収束覚束ず
海流汚染処理すべもなく

The resolution
Of the nuclear accident
Is unpromising
There isn't yet any means to deal
With marine pollution

礫下に埋もれし母の亡骸に
縋りし子らに波音哀し

The pounding of waves
Sound sorrowful to children
Clinging to the dead body
Of their mother buried deep
Under a heap of rubble

砂浜の夜道を急ぐ母を待つ
父亡き子らに海鳴り悲し

      The roars of the sea
      Sound weird and sorrowful to
      Fatherless children
      Who wait for Mother hurrying
      On the sandy beach at night

大津波襲いし父母の姿なく
捜せる子らに夕闇迫る

      Nowhere could be found
      Parents assaulted on by
      The big tsunami
      The dusk was near at hand on
      Their children looking for them

夕暮れの岸辺に寄せる潮騒に
とけゆく君の口笛哀し

  Your whistle sounded
  Pathetic which was merged
  Into the roar of
  The sea waves boring down on
  The seaside of the evening

避難所の夕闇迫る街角で
古里思い老女佇む

  At the street corner
  Of the emergency site
  The dusk gathering
  In memory of her home
  An old girl remains standing

除染土の埋もれし家の庭先に
可憐にそよぐ春の花々

    Close to my garden
    Where decontaminated
    Soil was buried
    Many kinds of spring flowers
    Fluttered in the gentle breeze

深々と雪降る庭に寒椿
枝もたわわに紅匂う

    In the garden where
    Snow is falling thick and fast
    Crimson camellias
    Which are heavy with branches
    Are in full bloom fragrantly

震災で乱れし部屋の片隅に
昔読みにし本の温もり

In the nook of my room
Confused by the Great Earthquake
I feel the warmth of some books
Which I had read many times
When I was a little boy

復興の兆しが見えぬ古里で
瓦礫に埋もれ成す術もなく

In the native place
No signs of reconstruction
Are to be seen yet
Buried in lots of debris
There is no means for doing

妻子とも別れて過ごす被災地で
アパート暮らし寒さ身に染む

In the stricken zone
I stay separately now
From my wife and child
Leading a life in a flat
The cold bites me to the bone

雪降る夜仮設住居でただ独り
亡き妻偲び熱燗を飲む

In makeshift housing
Without any amusement
In a friendless life
Remembering my late wife
I drink hot sake alone

古里で楽しき時を妻と子と
過ごせし我が家見る影もなき

In the native place
I passed a very good time
With my wife and child
Now few remains of our house
Which keep its framework only

安達太良の雪解け水が山里の
汚染を流す術となりしや

Will it be possible
For snow- melted water of
Mt. Adatara
To drain contamination
Spread among mountain's villages?

春遅く安達太良山の雪解けて
山の恵みを取り戻せしや

The piled- up snow of
Mt. Adatara melted
Late in spring
Did the mountain recover
The rich blessings of nature?

白鳥の飛来し川辺風強く
汚染し餌を食むや哀しき

In the riverside
Where many swans come flying
The cold wind is strong
It is pathetic for swans
To eat some polluted prey

白鳥が汚染し空に悠々と
飛び立つ姿朝焼けに映え

A flock of swans are
Flying off from the river
Into the foul sky
Whose graceful figure has glowed
In the rosy sky of dawn

目に見えぬセシウム恐れ乳飲み子の
行く末案じ涙零れる

Being in fear of
Invisible cesium
Worrying about
The future of her suckling
Tears get spilled from Mother's eyes

「この砂に触っていいの」と聞きし後も
砂とたわむる子の姿なき

      We can't see any
      Innocent scene of children
      Who are trying to play
      With sand after asking "Can
      I touch such foul sand as this?"

「このりんご線量計で測ったの」と
確かめてなお食べぬ子らあり

      There are some children
      "Who ask us if this apple
      Has been checked with
      A dosimeter?" and won't
      Try to take a bite of them

避難者に「放射能うつすな」と
揶揄する子らの心痛まし

How piteous and
Heartbreaking may be children
In some districts who
Banter evacuees not to
Give radiation with them!

年老いて内部被曝を測りしも
残りし余命幾ばくもなく

In my older age
I have had my internal
Exposure measured
For the first time in my life
I haven't much longer to live

原発の事故の汚染土貯蔵する
フレコンバッグが不気味に映えて

Flexible container bags
Which store soil polluted by
Nuclear accidents
Are set aglow eerily
By the sun in the evening

復興の見通し暗き被災地で
「負けねど！津波」意気や頼もし

In the stricken zone
Prospects for recovery
Are hard to see yet
The people's will is hopeful
We can endure Tsunami!

復興の足音響く被災地に
匂い懐かし庶民派グルメ

The gourmet cuisine
Of masses reminds us of
A nostalgic smell
In the stricken zone footsteps
Of recovery are heard

北限の信夫の里の柚の実が
枝もたわわに朝焼けに映え

The yuzu fruits of
The hamlet of Shinobu
Heavy with branches
In the Northernmost limit
Set aglow by the red dawn

由緒ある信夫の里の紅葉が
色鮮やかに秋空に映え

The crimson leaves of
The hamlet of historic
Sinobu forest
Set aglow by the fall sky
Brilliantly in colour

小鳥鳴く「小鳥の森」の山沿いに
色とりどりの花咲き乱れ

Along the mountain trail
Of 'the forest of birds'
Where small birds warble
Flowers of diverse colors
Bloom in riotous profusion

秋の日に銀杏並木の散策路
落ち葉踏みつつ歩き回りて

In the autumn's day
I wandered alone around
The walking street of
A row of maiden-hair trees
Trampling down the fallen leaves

晩秋の夕日に映える花見山
日が暮れかかり先を急ぎて

So late in Autumn
Hanamiyama set aglow
By the evening sun
Because light was falling down
I had to make haste at home

秋の日の日差しを浴びて山里の
人無き道を一人彷徨う

　　　　Bathed in the sunshine
　　　　Of the autumn of the year
　　　　I wandered alone
　　　　Along the lane without men
　　　　Of the hamlet among mountains

山裾の露天風呂から見る夜空
煌めく星が美しく映え

　　　　The fine sky at night
　　　　Looking from the hot spring-spa
　　　　At the mountain's side
　　　　A lot of glittering stars
　　　　Look bold beautifully

吾妻峰に夕日輝き半月が
南の空に霞み浮かびて

> The declining sun
> Glitters in Mt. Azuma
> And a half-moon is
> Floating dimly and lightly
> In the southern firmament

冬日射す仮設の庭の片隅に
椿数輪紅匂う

> Some small camellias
> Are in bloom fragrantly
> In the nook of the garden
> Of our temporary house
> The winter sun is shining

如月の草木根が張る被災地に
豪雪襲い春まだ遠く

     In February
     Heavy snows hit the district
     Stricken by disasters
     Trees and plants have spread their roots
     Spring has been still far away

窓越しに見る曇天の冬景色
墨絵のような風景に見え

     The wintry scene of
     A cloudy weather we look
     Through a room's window
     Looks like a lovely landscape
     Drawn in an Indian-ink

早春の残雪映える吾妻峰に
沈む夕日が明るく映えて

In Mt. Azuma
The lingering snow looks bold
So early in spring
The setting sun sets aglow
Brightly in the Western sky

信頼と優しさ胸に避難者が
集いし部屋に春忍び寄り

Hugging to our hearts
Trust and tender-heartedness
Spring is creeping up
On the room we gather
With hopeless evacuees

コロナ禍に地震災害雪降りて
冷たき風に春まだ遠く

      The corona's curse
      Has spread all over Japan
      The snow has fallen
      And the great earthquake occurred
      Spring is far for the cold wind

コロナ禍の桜前線北上し
桃源郷に桜綻ぶ

      The cherry-blossom
      Frontline of coronas curse
      Is going north step by step
      Cherry-blossoms start blooming
      In the earthly paradise

春風にコロナが街を徘徊し
賑わう街が閑散となり

　　The coronas have
　　Been wandering in the street
　　Blown by the spring's wind
　　The streets were deserted and
　　Calm in the prosperous street

晩秋に映える夕日がコロナ禍で
沈む心を奮い立たせて

　　The declining sun
　　Set aglow late in autumn
　　Summons up my heart
　　Being so buried in grief
　　Because of corona's curse

古き日の面影残す街並みも
時代の波に抗す術なく

    The old townscape which
    Has preserved the appearance
    Of the by-gone days
    There's no help for resisting
    The great current of the times

百年余続きし老舗倒産し
夜逃げのごとく里を追われる

    The old shop which lasted
    For a hundred went bankrupt
    Its owner's family
    Were expelled from its hometown
    As if running off at night

絶望に沈みし心鞭打ちて
破産の家を再興せしや

By encouraging
My heart plunged into despair
By which way can we
Reestablish our old house
Which has been declared bankrupt?

「がんばろう！」の旗街中にはためくも
冷たき風に木々咽び泣き

The flags, 'Let's stand out firm!'
Have been fluttering
In the crowded streets
Many trees have been sobbing
In the cold and biting wind

被災者の分断・亀裂乗り越えて
連帯の旗いかに立てしや

Getting through the split
And rift between evacuees
How should we rally
Together under the flag
Of our solidarity?

2．心貧しき青春の思いを胸に
—Keeping Memories of My Poor Youth in My Heart—

年老いて心貧しき青春の
思いを胸に短歌を詠みて

        In my olden age
        Keeping good memories of
        My poor younger days
        In my heart so profoundly
        I composed lots of tankas

感性と知性を鍛え夢多き
未来に向けて一歩踏み出す

        I will cultivate
        My great sensibility
        And intelligence
        I will take my step towards
        My future rich in my dreams

若き日に高き目標設定し
その達成に努力続けて

In my younger days
I set my higher purpose
I continued to
Make my strenuous efforts
To establish its purpose

長男に生まれた業を断ち切りて
われ進学の決意を固めり

Breaking off my fate
I was born the eldest son
Of a large family
I determined to go on
To the University

家業継ぐ責任ありと言う父に
進学すると意思を伝えし

> To my father who urged me
> To have my duty to take
> Over business
> I conveyed my will to go
> To the University

文学は無益の学という義兄に
学問の意義いかに説きしや

> My brother-in-law
> Said literary study
> Useless in living
> How could I persuade him to
> Understand its importance?

売り上げで金二百円積み立てて
義兄学費をわれに送れり

> My brother-in-law
> Reserved two hundred yen
> A day and sent me
> All my expenses during
> The period of schooling

なけなしの金をはたきて『チボー家』の
原書を手にし心昂ぶる

> I got excited
> To get the original
> Work of Les Thibault
> By spending what little money
> I had in my poor young days

勉学の時間バイトにとられても
寸暇を惜しみ原書紐解く

I was so busy
Working part-time that I had
Little time to study
Yet I tried so hard to read
Books in the original

若き日に愛を詠いしアラゴンの
原書を読みし君ぞ恋しき

In my younger days
My heart yearns for the lady
Who read some poems
In the original text
Aragon wrote about love

エルザへの愛を詠いし詩の本に
ほのかに郁る君の面影

　　　I feel nostalgia
　　　For your smell remaining
　　　In the old book
　　　In which Aragon composed
　　　Some poems of love for Elza

ただ独り一心不乱に本を読む
君の瞳に知性溢れる

　　　Her beady eyes were
　　　Deeply full of her wisdom
　　　And intelligence
　　　While she was intently absorbed
　　　In reading only alone

情熱を抑えし君の微笑みに
孤独に耐える知性漂う

　　　With a smile on your lips
　　　Repressing your feeling of
　　　Passion you project
　　　An air of intelligence which
　　　Bears your life in solitude

青春の愛の詩集を形見にと
嫁ぎし君を想い儚む

　　　I pitied for you
　　　Knowing that you got married
　　　Keeping the love poems
　　　Written about adolescence
　　　As a memento of youth

若き日の思いを胸に懐かしき
君が歌えし「白いブランコ」

Keeping memories
Of my young days in my heart
You sing the song of
The excellent 'White Trapeze'
I feel so nostalgic for

美しい豊かな声でシューマンの
「詩人の恋」を君が歌えて

You sing the song of
'The love of poet' composed
By Robert Schumann
In your very beautiful
And eloquent voice of song

君が剝くりんごに残る指痕の
ほのかな香り心慰む

　　　I've been comforted
　　　By the faint agreeable scent
　　　Of your finger marks
　　　Remaining on the apple of which
　　　You cut off the skin

思い出を語らいながら君が注ぐ
ワインの香り心身に染む

　　　I felt deeply bathed
　　　In the sweet fragrance of wine
　　　You poured in my glass
　　　Talking your dear memories
　　　Of your agreeable young days

若き日に共に読みにし古本に
残りし君の薫り懐かし

      I feel nostalgic
      For your agreeable scent
      Which still now remains
      In the used book I had read
      With you in my younger days.

教職の道に進むか迷いし後
大学院へ進む決意し

      After I wavered
      About whether to enter
      Teaching profession
      I made up my firm mind to
      Proceed to graduate school

六〇年安保の波に身を委ね
社会変革われも夢みし

I gave myself to
The demonstration against
The Security Treaty
In the sixtieth I dreamed
Social revolution too

3. 政治的季節の中で
―In the situation of the political season―

耳目引く世界遺産になりし後も
富士の裾野に軍旗はためく

> After being placed on
> The World Heritage List which
> Catches the public eyes
> Army flags are fluttering
> At the foot of Mt. Fuji

戦争の足音響く街角で
平和を願う署名を集め

> In the street the sound
> Of the war reverberates
> All over Japan
> We collected many signs
> Hoping for peace in the world

自衛隊を国防軍に再編し
戦争できる国へと変える

The Authority
Realigns the Self Defense Forces
Into National Security Forces
And changes Japan into
A nation engaging in war

軍隊の靴音高く改憲の
旗手鮮明に秘密保護法

The footsteps sound high
Of military forces
The Espionage Law
Makes clear a flag-bearer for
Constitution's revision

国民の秘密保護法反対の
声なき声に聞く耳もなく

The Authorities
Won't lead their ears to the voices
Of the dumb millions
Who take a firm stand against
The Secret-protection Law

妻と娘が「秘密は駄目よ」と
誓いし日秘密保護法奇しくも通る

On the same day that
Wife pledged to her daughter,
"No secret at all"
The Secret-protection Law
Passed through the Diet oddly

ネオナチの影忍び寄る十字路に
アンネの像毅然と立てり

The Anne's statue
Stands bravely and dauntlessly
At the street's crossroad
Where the gloomy shadow of
Neo-Nazism steals up to

プーチンの侵攻進むウクライナ
平和を求め民衆決起し

In the Ukraina
Puchin went on to invade
A lot of people rose up
And resisted his oppression
Dauntlessly in search for peace

ひめゆりの悲劇を胸に沖縄の
平和の誓いいかに伝えん

Keeping in our hearts
The tragic destiny of
The Star Lily Nurses
How can we convey the pledge
Of peace of Okinawa's people?

民族の誇りを武器に団結し
平和の砦名護の闘い

The Nago's struggle
The stronghold of peace goes on
By their union
With their national pride
As the weapon of their battle

権力の飽くなき魔の手跳ね返し
踏みにじられた誇り力に

Okinawa's people repulsed
Persistent devil's hands
Of the power and struggled
With their suppressed pride
As the force of their action

数千人集いし秋の集会で
脱原発の決意を胸に

In the meeting where
Thousands of people gathered
In autumn we made
Our fresh determination
Of denuclealization

原爆の悲劇を胸に憲法の
平和の理念いかに擁護し

Keeping in our hearts
The tragedy of A-bomb
How should we defend
The idea of true peace
Of the Constitution now?

生涯を世界平和と反戦に
微力を尽くす決意新たに

I have just renewed
My fierce determination
To do what I can
For international peace
And antiwar all my life

4. 高齢期を迎えて
―Hailing a Senior Citizen―

教育と研究一途に五十年
悔い残せしも心爽やか

     I have devoted
     My space of fifty years to
     Education and studies
     I feel invigorated
     Though I retain some regrets

生涯を捧げしわれの研究に
社会的意義どれだけありや

     How much can we find
     Social significance
     In my literary study
     To which I have been
     Dedicated through my life?

老妻と喜寿を祝いて初孫を
抱きて余命いくばくありや

    I celebrated
    My 77 birthday with
    My old wife and held
    My first grandchild in my hands
    How long will my years remain?

婆ちゃんの肩揉む孫の優しい手
その温もりに涙零れて

    The tender hands of
    Her granddaughter massaged
    Both of her shoulders
    Whose drops of tears set spilled from
    Her eyes over her warm hands

おじいちゃん大好きだよと孫娘
優しい声に心ときめく

My granddaughter says
'I like granpa very much'
My heart has beaten
By her tender and lovely
Tone of never-failing voice

コロナ禍で二年余会えぬ孫娘
その生長を夢に描きて

I have no chance of
Meeting my daughter-in-law
Living far away
Because of corona's curse
I draw her growth in my dream

未知の地で我を導く人無きて
九十九島の孤島を旅し

      In the unknown land
      No one exists who leads me
      I go on a trip
      Around Kujukushima
      The isolated island

定年後生きる目標設定し
実り豊かな余生を生きて

      I have set my aim
      Of life after I retired
      I have lived my life
      Of my own remaining years
      Which prove to be so fruitful

短歌とは森羅万象表現し
心伝える素敵な魔術

      Tankas signify
      The marvelous magic by which
      We can express all
      The creatures in nature and
      We can convey our true heart

震災を短歌に詠みて英訳し
英米人に記念に贈る

      I composed tankas
      About the greatest earthquake
      And put them into English
      Which I gave as my souvenir
      To English-speaking people

中欧の一流オペラ招聘し
復興支援に『魔笛』を演じ

　　　We have invited
　　　The first-class opera troupe
　　　Of Central Europe
　　　Who has played "the Magic Flute" for
　　　Our support for revival

中欧の一流歌手と即興で
『ドン・ジョバンニ』の初舞台踏む

　　　I made my debut
　　　Adlib on the fine stage of
　　　"Don·Giovanni"
　　　With the first-class opera
　　　Singers of Central Europe

爽やかな秋風の吹く被災地で
復興祭が被災者鼓舞し

        In the stricken zone
        The balmy autumn wind blows
        Lots of refugees
        Are mustered up courage by
        The revival's festival

伝えよう心の声を被災地で
豊かな明日を育むために

        Let us deliver
        The true voice of our own heart
        In the stricken zone
        To foster the rich future
        Of all the generation

あとがき

　この度、2011年3月中旬に経験した未曾有の東日本大震災・原発事故を題材に創作した英詩や英語短歌を書籍として纏め、出版することになった。当初、書籍の出版の是非を巡って、何人かの友人や知人に相談した。幸い、相談した方々が書籍として出版することに賛成してくださった。出版する以上、できるだけ多くの読者に読んでいただき、作品に対する率直な意見や評価を仰ぐのも意味があるのではないかと思い、出版する決心をした。

　日本の出版事情が大変厳しい折、この種の英詩や英語短歌を出版することが可能かどうか、その判断を仰ぐために、インターネットで出版社を調べ、文芸社が適切なのではないかと判断し、作品を送付した。文芸社出版企画部リーダーの青山泰之氏から、出版企画部の6人の編集委員が作品を読み、出版が可能かどうか慎重に検討し、その結果、「英語・日本語からなる詩集、短歌集」の「表現の美しさが印象深い」との「作品講評」を添えて、出版可能と判断した旨の返事を頂いた。青山氏がまとめてくださった作品に対する具体的な評価・コメントが、筆者の創作意図を汲み取った内容で、出版する意義があるのではないかと判断した大きな理由となった。

　序文でも触れたように、英文学を研究の対象とする筆者は、これまで詩や短歌を創作した経験がなく、この度創作した英詩

や英語短歌も詩的情緒や抒情性が豊かであるとは言い難く、拙い作品に過ぎないのではないかと憂慮している。その憂慮を断ち切り、自作の英詩や英語短歌を公表する契機となったのは、後期高齢の年齢になって経験した東日本大震災・原発事故を題材に、世界文学会誌『世界文学』の特集「災害と文学」に原稿を執筆してほしいとの編集委員会の要請があったからである。『世界文学』には、震災のルポルタージュとして掲載したが、その後、このルポルタージュの韻文で執筆した「早春賦2011─東北の荒れた大地で」を英訳し、新英米研究会誌"New Perspective"に掲載した。初めて創作した英詩を研究会員がどのように評価するか心配したが、幸いその評価が筆者の期待以上に高いことに励まされた。序文で触れたように、東日本大震災と原発事故を題材に初めて詠んだ短歌が「朝日歌壇」（馬場あき子選）に入選し、「朝日新聞」に掲載された。この短歌とその後に詠んだ短歌３首を英訳し、『新英語教育』（高文研、2020年１・２月号、No.605、No.606）に掲載した。引き続き、東日本大震災、若き日の思い出、現今の危機的政治状況、高齢期の現況を題材に76首の短歌を詠んで英訳した。下田市在住の歌人・長友くにさんと地域誌編集責任者の森彪氏の計らいで、この76首の英語短歌を秦野市の地域誌『緑のはだの』に掲載した。更に、最近詠んだ短歌４首の英訳を『新英語教育』（高文研、2022年10月号・No.638、2023年１月号・No.641）に掲載した。

　英詩や英語短歌を創作し、書籍として出版するに至るまでの経緯は以上の通りである。この度の書籍出版の労をとってくだ

さった文芸社の皆さんに心から感謝したい。

　英詩や英語短歌を出版する以上、在日の英米人を含む英語を母語とする第一言語話者（Native speaker）にもぜひ読んでほしいと願っている。国籍を問わず、この書籍の読者の方々には、『英詩・英語短歌集』に関して忌憚のないご意見・ご感想をお寄せ戴ければ幸いである。

安藤　勝夫

1937年4月　福島県矢吹町に生まれる
1956年3月　福家島県立白河高校卒業
1961年3月　東北大学文学部英文科卒業
1964年3月　東北大学大学院文学研究科修士課程修了
1964年4月　八戸工業高等専門学校講師
1966年11月　福島大学助手
1967年4月　福島大学講師
1970年4月　東北大学兼任講師（非常勤）就任（2007年3月辞任）
1974年4月　福島大学助教授
1976年10月〜1977年9月在外研究員（英国London University 留学）
1982年4月　福島大学教授
2003年3月　福島大学定年退職、同大学名誉教授
2004年4月　東日本国際大学教授
2008年3月　東日本国際大学定年退職、同大学名誉教授
2008年4月　東日本国際大学嘱託教授
2013年4月　東日本国際大学退職

【主な著書・翻訳書】
『英米文学─名作への散歩道〈イギリス篇2〉』（トマス・ハーディ『日陰者ジュード』）（三友社出版 1983年）
編著『北国に芽ぶく英語教育（英語教育実践風土記3）』（三友社出版 1984年）
共訳書『民族主義・植民地主義と文学』（法政大学出版局 1996年）
編著『なぜ「日陰者ジュードを読むか」─ハーディ文学の新しい鉱脈を探る─』（英宝社 1997年）
共著『シティズンシップ教育の展望─ラッグの思想とコア・カリキュラム』（ルック 2006年）
共編 Comprehensive Readings for Culture：Introduction to Cultural Studies（英宝社 2005年）他

著者プロフィール

安藤 勝夫 （あんどう　かつお）

福島大学・東日本国際大学名誉教授

1937年４月　福島県矢吹町に生まれる
1964年３月　東北大学大学院文学研究科修士課程修了
1982年４月　福島大学教授
2003年３月　同大学名誉教授
2004年４月　東日本国際大学教授
2008年３月　同大学名誉教授

（詳細なプロフィールは前ページに掲載）

早春賦　**Ode to the Early Spring**
英詩・英語短歌集　A Collection of English Poems and Tankas

2023年７月15日　初版第１刷発行

著　者　　安藤　勝夫
発行者　　瓜谷　綱延
発行所　　株式会社文芸社
　　　　　〒160-0022　東京都新宿区新宿１−10−１
　　　　　　　　　電話　03-5369-3060（代表）
　　　　　　　　　　　　03-5369-2299（販売）

印刷所　　図書印刷株式会社

ISBN978-4-286-24250-7